TO LOVE

&

TO CHERISH

Oluseyi Gabriel Akinyemi

Published in the United Kingdom by Greenlife Publishers
as a softback and e-book in March 2020.

Copyright © Oluseyi Gabriel Akinyemi

ISBN: 978-1-9162664-7-6

Dedication

This piece of work is dedicated to women enduring domestic violence in their marriages. It is also dedicated to people who are struggling with childhood traumatic experiences. I hope this book would help them see the light at the end of their tunnel.

Preface

To Love and To Cherish is my first published work. I got my inspiration from counselling lots of young people in different parts of the world.

This book teaches pure marital wisdom in relatable form. I wrote this short prose, hoping it will inspire the 21st century couple on how to work around their marital issues, how to make a marriage work, how not to be judgmental, and how to accommodate each other's flaws.

I wrote my first piece fifteen years ago, and since then, I have been a freelance writer writing short stories and drama series.

To Love and To Cherish is going to inspire young and aspiring couples, especially those who see marriage as a battleground and many who propagate gender wars through extreme feminist agenda.

This book teaches forgiveness, accountability, and karma in a relatable form. It helps us see why we should not give up on people or write off anyone in life.

It is simply a fictional work of the author. Any coincidence with any true character is not intentional.

Acknowledgement

First of all, I am grateful to the Master of the Universe, which most religions in the world call God.

My life has been shaped by great values of love, integrity, uprightness, and compassion. And all these wouldn't have been possible without a solid foundation laid by my parents – Gabriel and Temidayo Akinyemi. I am grateful I had the opportunity to be raised by this wonderful pair in this lifetime.

Special thanks to my amazing siblings, Shola (Pappy), Tolutoludo and Bisi, Segun and Iretioluwa Akerele, I would like to say a big thank you to you guys because you have been ever-loving and supportive and have always believed in me.

I remember with fondness my friends who also double as my super-duper strategic team; Jake, Peter, Samson, and Hector, your steadfast support and confidence inspires me in many ways.

I am deeply grateful to the thousands of people that I have had the opportunity to counsel in this lifetime.

It has been a great opportunity not just to give to my world, but also to learn from all of you.

Introduction

Most marriages fail between the first and the fifth year. Statistics has shown that most spouses endure domestic violence in marriages, especially the womenfolk who think it's an act of love to endure marriage instead of enjoying marital bliss. The kids raised within this family who see their dad emotionally and psychologically abuse their Mum do not ever see anything wrong with abuse, and they are usually not comfortable with any relationship that is not abusive.

Through adaptation and learning, they tend to see violence, male dominance, and masculinity as a normal way of relating when they are eventually in a romantic relationship. Children subtly re-enact whatever value system their parents lay down for them.

They grow up to repeat what they see, and in most cases, they end up producing all that they have grown up with, even if they know intuitively that it is not right.

To Love and to Cherish is a book that would subtly pass that message, in such a very small way, or sometimes, in a big way. I am hoping that many readers can come to a place where they can transcend whatever challenges they might have faced while growing up.

In the words of a wise man, we all have a background, and we have a choice to grow up as individuals or simply let our background keep our backs on the ground.

Table of Contents

Prologue

Time was running out fast, and I felt my life was fleeing away. I woke up with a sickening feeling, and I could not figure out where I was. I just saw some handful of women spotting white gowns, some were fixing needles to my body looking agitated, and some, tapping my chest while others were walking away hurriedly as if in a haste to keep an appointment. I drifted back into a long sleep, and I wish I never woke up. I woke up for the umpteenth time, my heart was flooded with the memories of the past. It gushed out like the *Olumirin waterfalls* in Osun state, Nigeria. The time is present, but it was a few years earlier.

I would describe myself as a happy-go-lucky person, the type that can easily mix with anybody regardless of the sex, race, and colour. I wasn't born with a silver spoon, I didn't have the best education, no fancy clothes, no wonder on the wheels as cars, no intimate relationship with any girl, I am just the guy next door struggling to survive, working hard to get going, always positive and I try to see the bright side of life, and I was raised by my mum.

Before I grew up to the point of understanding and reasoning, my dad had bolted away with an unknown woman. For the first few years of my life, my mum had a particular phrase that she usually hum to my earshot "all men are the same, they are as cheeky as the devil, they come in subtle ways only for them to destroy a woman and move on." I never knew what that statement meant for a very long time, and I never bothered to know then because I was too young to decipher it. But as I grew older, I began to ask about my dad. I began to ask a series of questions, and I began to trouble my mum's tender heart. I worried her till she offloaded all her pains much to her relief, but to my detriment.

Down memory lane

Twenty-five years ago, it was in the town of Calabar, also known as Canaan land, the state capital of cross river state in the Coastal Southeastern region of Nigeria, the most populous country in Africa, otherwise known as the Giant of Africa. My dad, by the name Etim, the son of the village headmaster met my sweet mum during the annual youth festival in the village of Ntan Obu Ukpe in Eniong of Odukpani local government area in Cross River State.

Etim had just won the wrestling competition, and all the amiable young men were cheering him on. In a jiffy, he was lifted shoulder high, and songs of praise were rendered in his honour, while the maidens were dancing and clapping, moving their hips in sensual ways to the rhythm of the song. Etim sighted a lovely maiden who didn't join in the victory dance – he was shocked. As culture demands, whoever wins the annual wrestling competition automatically becomes the youth leader of the community regardless of his age or family background, and all youths must remain loyal to him as far as his tenure last. If the youth leader decides to compete again the following year and wins, then his tenure continues, and he can decide to re-compete in the annual youth wrestling competition until he attains the age of 30 years before he retires. Anyone above 30 years automatically becomes an adult in the community and sheds the toga of a youth. A beautiful maiden called Alice spots Etim from afar and frowns. Etim was angry at the audacity of the maiden's rudeness not to acknowlege him. He motioned to the young men carrying him, and he was brought down, he walked to her and asked why she has a frown on her face. Am I suppose to start dancing and rolling on the floor because you are now a youth leader, she asked sarcastically. Etim was infuriated by that statement and he slapped her immediately without blinking an eye. He looked at her and said, "My tenure has started, and I will deal ruthlessly with anyone that opposes me or my family." The maiden burst into tears, and she tried to fight back, but some young men standing aloof prevented her from incurring more wrath from Etim. Other maidens pacify Alice – the maiden that was just slapped by the new youth leader.

Alice's brother emerged out of the blues and challenged Etim's rash decision to slap his sister, Etim remained unruffled. A fight ensued between both of them, and within a twinkle of an eye, Alice's brother was on the dusty path. No one saw it coming, his face became swollen immediately, and he had received a deep cut near his mouth. Etim had dealt him some heavy punches and cleared him out of his way. He remained on the ground, moaning and nursing his wounds while fierce-looking young men were on guard to prevent any harm from befalling Etim. There was loud drumming and singing, wild and sexy dancing from the maidens while some others led Alice away. The palm wine jar was opened, and the kolanut was shared, drinking started in earnest, and Etim was taken round the village square. He was drinking heavily as he was being carried about, others joined him after the customary prayer was said to bless the palm wine. He ordered some young men to bring Alice, the maiden he just assaulted. The other maidens had led her away, and they were some distance towards the market square when the young men caught up with them panting, "Etim, the youth leader, wants you back at the ceremony ground immediately," the heftiest one thundered. The other maidens were scared stiff, Alice protested faintly, the other young men received a signal from their leader, and they bundled her back to the ceremony ground.

By this time, Etim was very sober, and his speech was hazy and incoherent. When he sighted Alice being bundled towards him, he barked at the young men to drop her down at once. They obeyed swiftly and mixed with the crowd. Etim fixed his gaze on

Alice, he looked at her round curves, and smiled gently, he kept his eyes on her for a while, he saw the innocence in her eyes and also gazed at her big bust for a long time much to the embarrassment of Alice and the other maidens watching from a distance. There were tiny little whispers going on in the background. Some said he hates her so much and he would beat her up, some others said he fancys her, all of this was going on amongst the ladies and the young men who were all speaking in hushed tones. Etim moved in calculated steps towards Alice, he tried to touch her cheeks, but she shoved him aside. He started apologizing profusely for assaulting her, his sweet, tender, and persuasive words were soothing to Alice, and most people could not hear what he was saying, but from time to time, Alice giggles and chuckles. He lifts her from the dust, arranges her dishevelled hair, pecks her cheeks, and they walk hand in hand like a couple, they walked far away into the night, giggling all the way and playing like love birds much to the dismay of the maidens. An intense argument ensued as soon as Etim and Alice disappeared from view, tempers flared, and clothes were torn into shreds by the maidens there. Many young men fed their eyes to their satisfaction that night after filling their stomach with much liquor. Some staggered away, and the few that tried to separate the maidens were overpowered, they resigned and left the maidens to their fates, but the fun-loving ones stayed back and fed their eyes until the fight ended and everybody dispersed. Three months later, Etim and Alice were married.

"I refused to heed the early warning signs" my mum lamented as she continued to take me down memory lane. The beatings were at first bearable before marriage, but they continued after marriage, and when I could not take it anymore, I left the city and ran back to our community," my mum sobbed. Her parents waded in, and she reluctantly went back to the city to continue living with my Dad. It is a taboo in her culture for a married woman to spend more than a night under her parent's roof, so the next day, she returned to the city. On getting back home, the door was ajar as she walked in, what she saw almost made her pass out. My Dad was in a romantic posture with another woman who was scantily dressed. She hurriedly dropped her luggage by the doorway, screamed, and ran towards them in a bid to free the woman from my dad's grip. Etim was angry at the confrontation; he held Alice by her throat and beat her black and blue. By the time Alice woke up, it was the day after, she had lost a lot of blood, and she was in premature labour. The doctors were relieved when she opened her eyes for the first time; a good Samaritan had rushed her to the hospital just in time. Three days later, she had a baby, and she said I was in the incubator for about six weeks. Some friends and relatives came to check on her, and they raised money to help offset the medical bills she incurred. When the doctors were satisfied that we were out of danger zone, we were duly discharged. Alice was battered physically and emotionally, it took weeks after her discharge for her wounds to heal physically, but it left a permanent scar on her mind. She got home, and she was traumatized when she discovered Etim had moved out of the house with no traces of him, the neighbours said they saw him come with a truck to move everything in the house, not even a pin remained in the house. Even Alice's properties were gone; it was heartbreaking to start from scratch. My mum recounts that these were the darkest days of her life. Her parents, friends, and well-wishers were there to comfort her and her new baby.

As I grew older, I was growing to hate my dad for all the pain he had inflicted on my mum. Years rolled by, one suitor came after another, but my mum turned them down. After a while, she started telling the suitors "I will rather get married to a lady than get married to a man." It was a statement from a hurting woman who had given everything to a man clothed in a "beast skin," borrowing the words of my mum. She had invested her all into the marriage just to make it work, but my dad treated her like an "animal" and eloped with a "prostitute." She devoted all her time to bringing up her only son. Her mum, who is my maternal grand mum, was living with us and stood by us through thick and thin until she died. My mum was devastated when my grandmum passed on, but life went on, she picked up the pieces of her life, and we relocated to Lagos state, the commercial capital city of Nigeria.

I grew up as a "Mummy's boy," at least that is what all my friends call me. My mum treated me like an egg and she overprotected me, but she did not fail to spank me when I misbehaved. She gave me her all, but this baffled me because I thought she would treat me the way my dad treated her, and going by the statement she utters regularly, one would have expected her to mete out worse treatment on me or even my male friends. Nevertheless, the reverse was the case; she showered and pampered me with love the way a young girl would pamper her man.

I grew up into the replica of my dad. My mum will, sometimes, taunt me by saying you have big eyeballs like Etim your dad; you are exactly like him in all aspect, the way you walk, talk, smile, and even dance, I pray you never imbibe his character." Those words exposed her fears and anxiety, and I cherished her even more. I made a deep resolution inside me never to hurt her or lay my hands on any woman. Meanwhile, I silently wished I could lay my hands on my Dad and avenge for my mum. I became fond of her and became the husband she never had. As I grew older, I played the role of my dad and the son. On one occasion, I had broken an older man's jaw for raining abusive words on my precious mum. We were in a traffic jam, and the guy drove dangerously and squeezed his rickety vehicle in front of ours. I got down immediately and questioned him for driving recklessly. He rained abuses on me and my mum, I could take the insult he rained on me but didn't find it funny when he insulted my mum. I dragged him out of his car and punched him in the face three times. My mum waded in, and other commuters came too, a crowd was gathering, but my mum apologized on my behalf and tempers were doused. As I wriggled my way out of the commotion, my mum sobbed silently, and my heart sank. She scolded me for fighting on her behalf, I had thought she would support me, or probably give me a peck on my cheeks as her custom was, but instead, my mum was sobbing like a baby, and she again expressed her fears about how I was towing the road of violence. I muttered, "Mum, what would you have expected me to do if I was your husband in that situation?" She continued sobbing, but I spoke on "I can't tolerate anybody insulting my mum, he could have laid his filthy hands on you if I didn't teach him a lesson and …" My mum interrupted me with a scream, and I was startled, I almost lost control of the car, " don't fight for me, please, this is the way your dad started by beating up different men and ladies outside all in the name of protecting me." She continued calmly " at first, I was very happy and felt secured until karma took its course, and he started laying his beastly hands on me." My mum later apologized for screaming at me and pecked me, I faked a faint smile, and we got home in one piece.

One sunny Saturday, my mum came back home from a wedding ceremony she attended in the company of her friends. I was hosting some of my friends in the living room, a male and two female friends, the girls were scantily dressed. I had bought gin and some juice too, and we were all tipsy before my mum came in. We were talking loudly, but we did not know, so we were oblivious of the fact that my mum was around. She walked in quietly with her friend. This was the first time I will ever see my mum bring a male visitor to the house. I was a little bit nervous, my friends greeted my mum, and she returned the greeting. I turned to my mum's guest and asked him with a stern look whom he was. He was embarrassed but smiled gently that he was her work colleague. I was not satisfied with the answer, so I kept on asking more questions until my mum rescued him, and asked me jokingly if I was a detective. At this point, the questions ceased, but I never knew I was a little drunk. Since my mum did not say anything about the gin and my semi-nude female friends, I felt she was okay with everything, so I went into my room with my friends, wore my jacket, and went out to buy more gin. On getting back, I hid the gin inside my jacket and went straight into my room. I didn't know that my mum was observing me from a distance, but she did not utter a word. A few hours later, when we came out of the room, I introduced my friends to my mum, she smiled and asked which one of them was my girlfriend. I just waved the question aside; my mum knew that I have been drinking. I was reeking of booze.

When my friends left, she warned me never to keep such friends again. She felt bad I had consumed a large volume of alcohol just the way my dad used to do, this made me feel bad and also sober at the same time. I just hate being compared to my Dad.

I told her I sincerely don't want to be like my Dad, she then said, one easy way not to end up like him is to stay away from alcohol. I agreed, and I promised never to use alcohol again. My mum was impressed, and she has a way of using the comparison with my Dad to make me do the things that she would want me to do.

I ran happily into my mum's room one Saturday after a night out with my friends the previous day, I had gained admission into Ahmadu Bello University, Kano, in the Northern part of Nigeria. At first, my mum rejoiced with me, but when she discovered I was going to be far away from her, she was sad. This was the first time I was having a major disagreement with my mum, we argued, and I refused to talk to her for days. I wanted her to shift grounds. My thoughts took over; "I think my mum was taking this too far, she still thinks i am a baby, and she always want things her way." The thoughts kept pouring in. I confided in my friends, and they gave various advice, all centred on my being firm and being a man.

At last, my mum saw that I was resilient, and she reluctantly allowed me to have my way. During those times, there was a detachment between my mum and myself for the first time in my life. We quarrelled for almost two weeks, and we did not speak to each other. I relocated to one of my closest friend's house, Moses, he fed me all through this period and introduced me to hard drugs. I also learnt how to smoke marijuana and cigarettes. The day I came home to pick more clothes, my mum accosted me, apologized, and said I could go to the University since that was what I wanted.

I was enjoying the company of the boys, especially Moses, and I was enjoying my new lifestyle of being able to consume lots of alcohol, smoke marijuana too, and enjoy the "highness" as we fondly call it. I also had it good with the ladies, and I didn't struggle to talk to any girl I wanted, many girls thought I was good looking; This was something that played well to my advantage with the ladies, and I experimented with random and casual sex with different girls. My mum noticed all this, and I noticed that she was disappointed. Still, I couldn't be bothered anymore just because I was tired of being a Mummy's boy, I desperately want to be my own man, to live my life just how I understood it, and those old ploys of "You are behaving just like Etim, your Dad." Oh, please, they don't work on me anymore. She noticed that too, and she decided to let me be, I was pleased with my new found independence. I was becoming a tough man. Three weeks later, I left for the University.

I came back after the first semester as a changed adult. I had gone to the University with a determination to enjoy every bit of the experience;

peer-pressure had taken the better part of me. When I saw my mum, she looked a little stressed up and worried. I burst into tears immediately. Loneliness had taken a toll on her, and I knew if I left her for another semester, she might slide into depression before I return home. I had wanted to transfer to the University of Lagos, but the University insisted I complete the whole session before I could do that. Therefore, I decided to forfeit my admission at Ahmadu Bello University and I waited for a whole year to process another admission into the University of Lagos, just so I could stay close to my mum and keep my promises to always be there for her. However, that decision proved to be fatal.

I had joined a secret cult when I was in the Ahmadu Bello University. Moses, my best friend, had invited me to a party a day after my matriculation; I innocently went in company of some female friends. I was drunk that day, I drove Moses' car to the party, he was a third year student of the University, and he was the brain behind my admission. He was also one of the leaders of the confraternity. I danced, had fun, and smoked marijuana at the party, and at a point in time, the party got to a crescendo, and the lights went out. I heard gunshots and people scampered out to safety, fierce-looking people in full black regalia rounded some of us up, we were beaten, stripped, and robbed of everything we had. They bundled us into a bus and drove us into a thick forest at the outskirts of the town. It seemed like an endless journey, but we eventually got there. Throughout the journey, the words of my mum kept ringing in my head, and I knew at that point that I had followed the wrong path. We were marched out of the bus, tortured, and initiated forcefully. We were more than twenty-five in number, but some died during the torture, and their bodies were hurriedly buried in the forest. I survived with some other men, our blood was taken, and we were confirmed as cult members. After that, the cult leaders who tortured us uncovered their faces, my friend, was amongst them. He had beaten me with a rod severely, and I never knew I would survive the ordeal, at a point, I prayed for death, but it was as if death could hear me speak loud because death fled that day, leaving me to my woes. After that experience, I never trusted him or anybody again, and I wished I had listened to my mum.

Moses and his friends came looking for me, and I told him calmly that my mum had health issues, and that I could not continue with my education again. He empathized with me and promised to keep in touch. Even if he suspected I was lying, he never showed it. I later went back to complete the second semester. I pressurized my mum to let us relocate after I started receiving threat messages on my phone. My mum said she had nowhere to go and that Calabar was out of it. I couldn't tell her about my ordeal in the past few months of our separation, and I felt we weren't that close again. I felt she didn't love me again, and I had also found succour with my friends and hard drugs. Therefore, I decided to tell my problems to friends, and they gave me all the wrong advice that could possibly last a man for a lifetime, cunningly packaged advice that seemed innocent and nice. Three months later, some unknown assailants attacked me on my way to purchase a University of Lagos entrance admission form. It was a few minutes after 7 pm, machete and axe were used on me, and I was severely disfigured, the excruciating pain was too much, and I passed out.

Present time

I woke up with a sickening feeling, and I could not figure out where I was. I just saw some handful of women spotting white gowns, some were fixing needles to my body looking agitated, and some were tapping my chest while others were walking away hurriedly as if in a haste to keep an appointment. I drifted back into a long sleep, and I wish I never woke up.

When I fully woke up sometime around midnight, I saw my dear mum smiling down at me the way the sun smiles radiantly on the earth, and I knew from that moment that I meant the world to her. The nurses came into my private ward again and motioned my sweet mum to come. I asked what the problem was; my mum did not want me to know, so she hurried out of the ward. Another nurse confided in me that my mum's blood pressure had gone up for the last three nights since I had been admitted, I learnt my mum is also a patient being attended to, even though she was acting like all was well. Tears welled up in my eyes because I felt I had put her through a lot, I was shocked to know that I had already spent three nights in the hospital and it seemed as if I had only been there for a few hours. I kept staring at the ceiling until I fell asleep.

The next morning, when I awoke, my mum was still fast asleep, I pecked her thrice, and she woke up like a baby. We discussed at length, I apologized, and my mum agreed with me that it was high time we left our former abode for a safer terrain on the outskirts of the city. I hate to see my mum cry and sad, though I had put her through a lot, I made a solemn promise to her that day not to bring any pain or sorrow to her, she held me closely and we were in a long embrace.

We were about to have breakfast when the chief physician whom we had been expecting since my admission in the hospital strolled inside the ward. I had sustained some major injuries and deep cuts on my head, but it was not life-threatening. The internal bleeding had stopped, and the machete blows on my back were healing faster than I expected. Thanks to the meticulous care I received from the nurses. My mum and I had been expecting the chief physician for the past two days who coincidentally turned out to be the one who rescued me from the jaws of death, I was told he singlehandedly fought my assailants, they fled, but he summoned courage and gave them a hot chase. At the end of the bridge across the cinema, he double-crossed the shortest of them, held him by the jugular and dealt him a deadly blow before he put a call across to the police officers. News later filtered in that three of them had been caught after the suspect confessed. I knew deep down that Moses is the brain behind all these.

Junior meets Senior

The time is present: The chief physician is a tall, lanky man, well built, and handsome with a boyish smile. I was told he didn't collect a dime, he offered to give me a free first-class treatment in his hospital, he saved my life, if he hadn't rescued me at that point, I might have died. He was carrying a stethoscope when he walked in, my mum was facing the wall when he walked in majestically, as my mum turned around with a smile of gratitude, she suddenly shouted "Etim," I thought she was referring to me. I promptly answered, but she pointed in the direction of the chief physician and stammered " Et... Etim"....my heart skipped a bit. I'm the carbon-copy of the chief physician, and I almost jumped out of my skin when I saw myself in him. My dad looks at my mum, mouth agape, my mum seems dazed, but with a forgiving smile, I stole a quick look at the chief physician, Etim senior beckons at Alice and Etim junior, lo and behold, and then....we were all in a tight embrace.

Cherish

She grew up in a remote area of Benue state, a little village filled with mountains and beautiful tree shrubs. The only familiar faces around her was that of her mum and her mum's relatives, who took good care of her and made sure she did not lack anything.

Her mum named her Cherish because she believed she was a gift from God to her despite all she went through. Her dad was a very known and popular name in the state, Cherish and her Mum only get to see his face on the pages of the newspapers or when he is speaking about political issues on the Television.

She grew up knowing her dad never wanted her because he wanted a male child. He didn't want to have anything to do with her Mum or with the child being that she was not a male child that he was expecting.

Cherish is a beautiful girl. Everybody around her admit that she is quite warm and pretty.

Her mum adored her so much. And she did everything humanly possible to show her love just so that she doesn't feel the void, or the psychological trauma of knowing fully well that she was rejected by her father.

Despite all this, Cherish always felt that she has been betrayed by the most important male figure in her life. She didn't understand how she was ever going to come to terms with ever finding the courage to love a man, and she was quite active and vocal in school to speak up against any form of oppression against women. She was loved and adored by all her school mates, and her teachers too.

Whilst she was in her first year in the senior secondary school, she faced yet another betrayal by her stepbrother who came back drunk one day and raped her. This was too much for her to handle and she just didn't know how to say this to her mum, or to anyone around her. She felt like her strength was waning, and that the world was just a dark place. Cherish was hurting inside, she felt broken and so small, yet she tried to carry on as if all was well. She has stopped been that vocal and very bold girl everyone knew, she was going through different roller coasters of emotions, simply hoping and wishing that this was just a dream, but alas, this isn't a dream, this is her new reality.

Her outstanding academic performance brought a lot of her classmates close to her as they either needed her to help with their course work or practical field works. Time passed by, she met Belinda, a kind young lady with a beautiful smile and kind heart. This endeared her to her, and they became best friends. They ate, washed, and slept together. The relationship was so strong that everyone around them thought they were lesbians, they always had to correct the narrative everytime amongst their classmates and everyone soon accepted them as best friends and soul sisters.

Love

Cherish and Belinda are now both students of the University of Ibadan, the University of Ibadan which is popularly known as UI is situated in Ibadan, Ibadan is a city in Oyo State, Nigeria and it is also the largest city in West Africa.

One sunny Sunday afternoon, Cherish was in a taxi on her way to the hostel, as soon as she came down at the bus stop, she met a charming young man who could not take his eyes off her, and for the first time in her life, she felt loved, and she felt that she was in love with him.

He walked towards her and introduced himself as Paul, a fellow student at the University. Paul was a third year student of the University while she was still a fresher. They talked for a few minutes, she was all full of smiles, very excited and simply felt comfortable around him. They exchanged phone numbers and went their separate ways.

Cherish ran off to the hostel out of excitement, she wanted to tell Belinda everything. She wanted her to know that she has experienced love at first sight. Belinda noticed Cherish was overtly excited, What's the gist girl? Seems like you have won a jackpot today, she said in a sarcastic tone. Cherish told her everything that happened, and how she felt when she met Paul. Belinda listened to the gist and was genuinely excited for her friend. I know you truly deserve to be happy she said, and I am happy to support you as long as this makes you happy, the two girls talked about dating, love and men until late into the night before they both slept off.

The next evening at about 9pm, Paul put a call through to Cherish who has been waiting anxiously for his call. They talked about a whole range of issues, and it felt like they had known each other for many years. Cherish looked at her phone and she realized that they had been on the phone for almost two hours, and in the twinkle of an eye, she told herself, I genuinely love this guy, this is real love.

Time had flown by quickly, even though Cherish and Paul had been dating for just about a year now, they both feel like they have been together for ages.

Paul had come to know everything about her, all she had gone through in the past, all of her pain, frustrations, and weaknesses; she was not holding back, she was more than happy to let him take the centre stage of her life.

Belinda on the other hand has had three different dates over the last one year, and none of the relationship seems to have worked well.

She admired Cherish and Paul, she always wished she had a relationship as beautiful as that of the two lovebirds.

The Betrayal

One bright sunny day, Cherish got a call from her mum, she was needed at home. There was a building project ongoing for a bit, the project is complete and its relocation time from the old apartment to the new house. Cherish left school for home, she asked if Belinda could come along, so she could help in moving out from the old apartment to the new. Belinda said she wouldn't be able to come simply because she had some pending course work to round up.

It's weekend, and it's a day to Cherish's birthday. Paul decided to pay her a surprise visit at the hostel. He got to the room and Belinda was there to welcome him. She explained to him that Cherish got a call from her mum that she needed to come help out in the house, he was surprised Cherish didn't inform him but when he brought his phone, he realized that she had dropped a text message for him to explain the situation.

The sky has been so dark and cloudy, the rain has started to fall. It was quite heavy and also very windy, one could hear some students running into the accommodation yard and screaming.

Paul was stuck here in the room with Belinda. Belinda asked Paul if he would like to take some London dry gin, Oh yes he said, I think this is a better way to handle this cold, it is a lot better than tea he said. They both laughed about it, and started drinking together.

This was practically their first time of talking extensively, they talked about campus life, dating, sex, society, movies and many more; Belinda also shared her relationship experiences with Paul. She thought that Paul was very unique, and many men out there play games in relationship. She also told him that she always wish she was with a man like Paul. The first bottle of gin was out of the way, Paul opened the second bottle, they were still talking, except that Belinda was feeling tipsy and also all cuddly now, and she was resting her head on Paul's shoulder. Paul was a little nervous for the first few minutes, they had stopped talking. It was really dark in the room with just a small candle light at the corner of the room, a slow soft music was playing in the background.

Paul looked into Belinda's eyes, and kissed her gently. It felt like this was that moment she has been waiting for, she kissed him hard, and that was just the beginning of their sexual exploration for the night. By around 2am, the rainfall was beginning to slow down, the second bottle of gin was finished, Paul and Belinda just had a wild sexual experience, Paul felt like he had never had anything like this before. By the next morning, he left the room around 5am. There was a feeling of guilt and a feeling of satisfaction, I really do have a better sexual chemistry with Belinda he thought to himself. I honestly do love Cherish, but I think she is sexually boring. Just maybe the rape may have been why she isn't sexually open and adventurous, I wouldn't even know. But one thing I do know is, the sexual experience with Belinda is the most beautiful thing I have ever experienced In this lifetime. I can't wait to get more of this, he said to himself.

Cherish returned after a few days, everything seems to go back to normal between the two love birds. Paul and Belinda have started to send erotic text messages to each other on a regular basis, and Paul was now a regular visitor to their room. Evelyn is the girl who lives next door to Cherish and Belinda, she isn't very close to either of them but they do say hello once in a while. Cherish was at the courtyard spreading her clothes, Evelyn was there as well trying to complete her laundry; then, Evelyn said to Cherish, I know Belinda is your bestie and you guys have been together for many years, however, I suspect Belinda and Paul are having an affair. I noticed that he was with her a few weeks ago when you were not around, I saw him sneak out of the room very early in the morning too. I have also noticed that he comes here many times when you are on campus, maybe you need to start observing them closely. I could also be your personal detective if you want, Evelyn said. Cherish was shocked to her bone marrows but she managed to let out a faint smile.

It is Friday, Cherish has been working closely with her private detective for about four weeks now. They have tried setting many baits for Belinda and Paul, but it seems this two are becoming smarter by the day. So Cherish told Belinda that she was going home for the weekend, and she also sent a text message to Paul as well to convey the same message to him.

Evelyn and Cherish had been just by the window in Evelyn's room waitng endlessly for Paul to show up. They have been there for about three hours and were both getting tired, Cherish was almost giving up on this again, and was almost beginning to doubt the cheating story. She walked away from the window to go sit on a chair in the room, the time is 9.15pm. Come Cherish, Paul is here, Evelyn said in a low tone. Cherish rushed back to the window, They both watch him as he walked through the hostel yard and climbed the stairs, and they also heard his footsteps as he walked down the corridor, finally, they heard when Belinda opened the door for him. Paul and Belinda have been at their sex escapade for just over an hour, the time is now 10.30pm. It was time for detective Evelyn and her client to strike. They walked out and they both stood by the door of Cherish and Belinda's room, and peeped through the keyhole. Paul and Belinda were both naked in bed, and they were in each others arms too.

Cherish handed the key over to Evelyn, Evelyn opened the room door all of a sudden. Paul and Belinda were caught in the act, they both froze and were speechless. Cherish couldn't stand the shock.....she slumped and passed out!

.

The Rebirth

Junior, the son of Etim and Alice, has moved back to another state to fulfil his life goals. He is the most popular relationship therapist in town. He is very empathetic and he can relate with his clients in such a way that almost everyone feel comfortable around him. With his upbringing, parental abuse, and neglect, he has been able to turn all of this disadvantage to an advantage, hence, giving him an edge over most of the psychotherapist in town.

This is Cherish' eighth session in eight months. Several years ago, she was advised to seek therapeutic intervention programs after she slipped into clinical depression and was placed on medication.

She dropped out of the University after the Paul-Belinda scandal. She relocated out of town completely to the city. But the scars of the betrayal never left her, and she was still wounded emotionally. Three other relationships followed suit rapidly, but it never lasted because she never really recovered from the emotional bruises from the previous one. She was hurting and she hurt every man she had a relationship with until they all got fed up of her insecurities and trust issues.

She lived with the guilt and the shame, she became suicidal, her mum had to seek help quickly.

A few years later, her mind is gradually being restored. All thanks to the medication and the therapy.

She looks extremely beautiful today, Junior thought. He kept scanning through this beautiful lady who sat gracefully opposite him. His heart beating rapidly, he smiles sheepishly with a boyish look. For a moment, he can hear his heart thumping. He grabs a glass of water to ease the tension.

You smell really nice Mr Johnson, she said whilst she kept her eyes fixed on him. His confidence seems to be boosted sharply by the compliment, he gets a grip of himself, he knew that this is not the same woman that was sat in his office a few months ago. She has been completely transformed and she now has a positive outlook about life.

The engagement

A few months later, they were out on a date. This is one other date from the countless dates they have had, but this other date wasn't just another date; it was a special date. The glass, the champagne, the romantic atmosphere, the waiters, and a few friends at the penthouse of the restaurant, the man on his knees, Cherish looking very gorgeous, Junior pops the question, and it's a big yes. He slips the 24-carat gold ring in her fourth left finger, gets up quickly, and kissed her gently on the lips while both were entangled in a long embrace. It was followed by a round of applause, giggles and cheers.

For better, for worse

"I, Etim Junior Johnson take you, Cherish Peters to be my lawfully wedded wife, to love and to cherish, from this day forward, for better, for worse, for richer for poorer, in sickness and in health, until death do us part," He smile as he completes the vow and she smiles at him through her veil.

"You may now kiss your bride, Mr Johnson," says the Clergyman.

Junior's heart races as he gently unveils his bride's face. She is so stunning, like a model gracing the front page of a fashion magazine. He gently bends over and places a soft kiss on her reddish lips. Cherish, in turn, embraced him tightly with tears of joy streaming down her face.

"Never leave me, Cherish." He whispers in her ear.

"I will never leave you," she whispers silently with tears of joy still pouring like rain torrents.

"I present to you the latest couple in town!" The Clergyman exclaimed excitedly.

The congregation claps cheerfully as the wedding ceremony comes to an end.

A decade later

Cherish silently tiptoes behind her husband. He was in his study, engrossed in the book he was reading. She chuckles, then gently covers his eyes with both hands.

"It's just you and I in this house, Cherish, how am I suppose to think there is someone else playing pranks on me" He said.

Cherish sighs and sits on the study table, "How do you figure me out so easily? She asks rhetorically. I can't even surprise you! That sucks a bit" she curls her arms around his neck.

"You are my wife, and we both in this house, or should I be expecting our dog to come put its hand over my face?" He playfully pokes her nose.

"But, you've been in the study all day, and I'm bored!" She rolls her eyes

"So, what kind of fun do you suggest we have then?" He sweeps her off the table in his arms.

"No! Not that kind of fun!" She hit him playfully till he puts her down

"Ok," so folding his arms on his chest, looking into her eyes, "So, what do you want us to do?"

"Not us; all I want is to play your playstation console, and you've hidden it again! Just give it to me, and you can continue with your reading, please." She blinks her eyes playfully.

"No way," he goes back towards his study chair and sits, "Not my play station console, the last time you played it, you played some games and lost all of them, so I lost the league cup that season."

"Why! You never let me touch it, and the only time you let me have it, you complained bitterly as if the console is your baby" She sulks.

"Oh well," rolling his eyes, "not like you've given

me a baby yet."

Cherish pauses for a moment. Did he just say that to me? She thought. The words struck her deep down, like a dagger thrust between her heart.

"You shouldn't have said that darling, that's so mean…" she blurts, her countenance changing.

"But it's the damn truth. The truth is as bitter as gall, hard to chew and bitter to swallow." He turns to face her, still sitting on the rocking chair.

"The truth? What truth? That I'm barren? You think I don't want us to have kids?" She cries.

"Don't get me wrong, and I'm not saying that…" He stands to face her now.

"Then, what are you saying, Junior? Tell me, what is the truth?"

"Let's not do this today… please. You can have the play station console and play all you want. It's tucked under the bed."

"You always do this… hurting me with your words, all the tests we have carried out over the years says we are both fertile and can have kids, so whose fault is it for our childlessness?" Her voice begins to shake

"Don't start, Cherish please."

"Tell me why you said those words to me! I want to know!"

"I'm kind of fed up, I'm upset, I want to be a dad, I want to have my own kids Cherish…"

" And you think I don't want kids too? Oh my God, you are just so pathetic." Cherish flares up totally, tension brewing in the atmosphere.

"Then, why can't you get pregnant, Cherish? It's over a decade now." Clenching his fist tightly and walking out of the study.

Cherish is in shock. She sits on the chair for some seconds, stands up again, and paces up and down the room, panting and in a reflective mood.

A few weeks later, inside the sprawling bedroom of the couple

"Junior, wake up please," blurts Cherish, tapping

him gently.

He opens his eyes, glancing at the alarm clock by the bedside, "its 2:00 am, Cherish…"

"It's urgent."

"I'm listening," He says drowsily.

"My mum says we should come for another series of tests. She said she has spoken to her general practitioner who has agreed to fix an appointment for us next month."

"What?" Junior opens his eyes wide, Your mum is in the United Kingdom for christ's sakes?"

"Let's just do it. We can spend some weeks there and also consider that time as some holiday or even as a romantic getaway. Let's just give it a shot, please."

"No. That would be rather expensive and…"

"It's my birthday today, and the only thing I want from you is this trip."

There is silence in the room. This is the third year in a row that he has forgotten about her birthday.

"I'm… I'm sorry, Cherish… It skipped my mind…"

"It always does." She said. She lays down on the bed, her back turned against him.

Wrapping his arms around her waist, he says "Sweetheart, I'm genuinely sorry…"

There was no response.

He sighs, "fine; we would go next weekend."

"Oh, yes" She became suddenly excited as if a switch has been turned on, her face now lightening up.

"Thank you, my baby." She hugged him.

Twenty-eight days later

Cherish jerks at the vibration of the phone in her pocket.

"Hi, Mum!" pressing the phone to her ear with her shoulders, wiping the washed dishes with her hands.

"Honey…"

"What is it, Mum?"

"The result…the result of the tests…" her my mum cried.

Cherish gently dropped the plate and the wiper, her heart racing…"Just say it, Mum…"

That night

"I can never have children, Junior…" Cherish cried.

Junior felt his world crash right in front of him, "W…what?"

"Mum called me today from the United Kingdom…she has the tests result, she posted it to me, so I picked it up from the post office today. Here you go, she hands him an envelope. He opens it hurriedly.

"Jesus Christ." Junior stands, arms akimbo, "b…but you never told me you didn't have a womb before we got married, you told me the surgeon said   Dilation & Curettage (D &C) didn't damage your womb. Now, have you been forging all the test results all these years, have you been conniving with the doctor to deceive me…have…?"

She cuts in "Don't bring my past into this."

Junior laughs hysterically and got serious almost immediately, "You are crazy. I married a crazy woman!"

Cherish looks at him in shock, like he'd lost his mind.

"The results say you can never have children and we both know that this has to do with the abortion you had before we met" he flared up,

You know we're screwed, right?

"Baby, we can adopt…" Cherish cried.

"Adopt? Wow!" He laughs again, "Obviously, I married a funny woman too. The damn baby will never be my flesh and blood. You are full of deceit, Cherish." He looks into her eyes. Cherish could see him fighting tears.

"Stop it, sweetheart…you are hurting me…" Cherish starts crying.

"Do you want to know what I'm thinking?" He says, looking at her with disgust, "I'm just thinking how on earth I'm going to stand seeing your deceitful face for the rest of my life."

"Cherish cries harder, "Don't give up, Junior…the results say I have a womb but just that my fallopian tube is blocked and it can be treated, so I have a womb. I can still carry our baby, but why are you judging me and peddling lies that I don't have a womb, didn't you read the test results?"

"Of course, I did, I am not giving up on having my baby, but I'm giving up on you. I'm trying to figure out why previous tests have never detected that your fallopian tube was blocked." Junior turns around to leave.

"Junior" She grabs his feet, "I'm hurting too…"

He frees himself from her grip and walks away.

A few months later

"Mum, he's not even talking to me. Suddenly, we are both strangers. He doesn't eat the food I prepare, he comes home late, and he hates me so much, and it's killing me. I'm confused to think that I showed him a fake test result just to test his love for me, it's truly hurting…"

"Why did you hide this truth from him? You've got to let him know the bitter truth.

A car horn blares outside.

"Mum, I've got to go… he's back."

"Baby, you've got to let him know. Show him all the original tests results and not the doctored ones."

"Bye, Mum" she ends the call.

Junior breezes into the lounge as he's about to walk past her.

"Junior," She holds him.

"I'm tired." He didn't want to look at her face.

"I know…can we talk for some minutes?" She tries to help him take off his jacket

"Look, what is it" He backs off.

"Do you hate me this much? Can't you even look at me in the eyes anymore? Can't you even stand my sight? Junior, it's me, Cherish, your best friend…" Her eyes are now misty.

"I'm in no mood for this." He turns to walk away.

"Don't you dare leave when I'm talking to you" pulling him back by his jacket, Just then some paper falls to the floor. Cherish quickly bends to gather them together, her hands shake, and her body became numb all over.

"D…divorce papers? Junior?" She searched his eyes.

"Answer me, goddammit!" She holds him by the collar of his shirt, crying.

"They are for you to sign. I want to be out of this fruitless marriage that is full of lies and deceit."

"Y…you what?" She slowly frees him from her hold.

"It's not going to work, Cherish, can't you see?"

"I can't believe you would think of divorce not to talk of even going this far…why are you so wicked!" She cries angrily.

"No! Why are you so wicked?" He fires back.

"Think about me for once. I am a man for Christ's sake, I want to be a dad, and you are about to deny me that for the rest of my life because of your stupid mistake, you never told me you had issues with your tube."

"What about me?! Have you stopped for once to think about what I'm going through?"

"It's your cross, carry it." Junior fixed his angry eyes on his wife.

"No, it's now our cross, and I am not signing those divorce papers! We vowed never to leave each other!"

"Isn't it better, Cherish that you save yourself more hurt and sign these papers than to see another woman move into this house before your very eyes?" He said with a tone of sarcasm.

Her heart thumps, "What?"

"You heard me… another woman who can help start a family. So, save yourself the stress and sign the damn papers. I need it tomorrow." He turns around to leave for the umpteenth time.

"She still can't carry your baby" she cuts in.

"Not all women had abortions. Not every woman is as careless as you." He scorns.

"You are the one who can't give me a child!" Cherish screams.

Junior stops in his tracks, he turns around and walks towards her. "Whatever your plan is, it won't work."

"I told you I could never have a child because it's you who can't make me pregnant."

"Shut up! Shut up, Cherish! What the hell are you saying?" He shakes her violently

"You are sterile … the doctor says you have erectile dysfunction, you can never make a woman pregnant…" Cherish burst into tears.

Junior gasps, losing his balance.

"My mum called me to give me the news. I was shattered, I felt like my world was over, but more importantly, I thought of you. I thought of what the news could do to you, I thought of the best way to tell you… never for once did I think of leaving you. I bore your insults, your scorn, because of my past. It was so easy to judge me and think of yourself. I am the one who is hurting. I am the one who should sign some miserable divorce papers, but I thought of you, and I hoped for a miracle. I thought of my vow to you when we walked down the aisle, In sickness and in health remember?" She smiled through her tears, "all of a sudden, you are as weak as a baby. Looking in your eyes, I can see you suddenly have lost all your guards." She hands him the original test results.

"Cherish…" he falls on his knees, shattered as if he has been struck by a thunderbolt.

"No!" She quickly falls on her knees too, "No, Junior…" She couldn't bear to see him cry

"I'm…I'm infertile, " he cries, "What is left of me?" Avoiding her gaze.

"Junior please." She holds his face, "I understand…it has been so hard for me…I have put myself in your shoes since the first day I received the devastating news."

"You don't deserve this; you deserve better. I can't believe I scorned you all along; please let me leave you."

"No." She shook her head, "You are my husband. I won't leave you. I won't let you leave me. I believe in miracles."

"I'm doomed…Cherish I'm doomed…"He allows his wife to take him in her arms and on her shoulder, they both cried like little children.

The morning after

Cherish gently opens her eyes, looking beside her bed, …it was empty. She quickly sits up on seeing a note carefully placed on the bed. Hands shaking, she opens the letter to read.

"Dear Cherish,"

I cannot bear the shame. I have maltreated you, yet you love me still, you chose to be with me despite my condition. To think that you knew all along and you never for once gave me a clue that it is my fault makes me think I am so unworthy of you. I love you and I want you to start another life with a man who can make you happier. I'm torn, Cherish, and all I ask is your forgiveness. I have always loved you, and if you truly love me, then please start your life over again…without me. I am truly sorry for disappointing you."

Junior

Cherish couldn't control the tears. She couldn't think straight anymore. She picks her cell phone, shaking.

"Hi Mr Johnson's office, please."

"Hi Shane…" she cries, "Have you seen my husband today?"

"No…no ma'am, we've been expecting him at work. He has a presentation fifteen minutes from now."

"Oh, God…God…" Cherish dips her hand in her full hair

"Is everything alright, ma'am?"

"Thank you" She ended the call.

She quickly got down from the bed, and in her pyjamas she runs into her car. She dials his number repeatedly as she drove off, but there was no answer.

2:00 pm

She speeds into Patrick's compound, a close friend to her husband.

"Patrick!" She bangs the door hastily till the door flings open.

"My God, Cherish, what's wrong?" Patrick holds her.

"It's…its Junior, have you seen him? Is he here?"

"No…I haven't heard from him in a week."

"Oh, God." She holds her hair.

"What's wrong?"

But she was already walking away into her car.

"Cherish!" He calls after her.

She zooms off.

4:30 pm

"Mum, Dad, I can't find Junior…I can't find your son…" She cried as she paces in front of her in-laws who look lost.

"You have to calm down and tell us what

happened" Junior's mum put her arms around Cherish.

Cherish burst into tears, "Please, Dad, could you try his number, maybe he'd pick your call?"

"Have you been to his office?" Etim Senior picks his cellphone and dials his son's number.

"Yes, I have checked everywhere he could possibly be."

"It's ok... calm down please" Junior's mum pets her.

"He's not picking. What exactly went wrong between you two?" Her father-in-law asks.

9:00 pm

Cherish was still in her pyjamas and on her way back home, exhausted and stuck in the traffic. She had told Junior's parents everything.

Cherish buried her head on the steering wheels, crying; she hadn't realized the green light had come on.

"Hey, get off the freaking road!" A driver cursed from behind her.

"God please, don't let him harm himself… keep him safe, and lead me to him, please God…" she quickly started the car and began to move.

Suddenly, she remembered the church where they wedded and took their vows. It was two hours from here. She made a U-turn and headed for the church, hoping to find some peace.

She tiredly got down from the car, drenched and exhausted. She trudged into the open entrance of the church. She paused for a moment; shocked…, it was Junior sitting at the front row of the empty church, facing the altar.

"Junior." She began to run towards him, happy, relieved that he was ok.

"Cherish?" He quickly stood as she approached him, "Cherish…"

They both ran into each other's arms. He hugged her so tightly.

"I've looked for you everywhere….thi--s was the last place I thought you'd ever be… I just came, and I saw you, Junior. I'm-- so happy you are ok" touching his face.

"I didn't know where else to go… It just feels like I can't face the world anymore…" he slowly releases her from his embrace.

"Take my hand." Cherish stretched out her hand, "C'mon, just take it."

Junior gently clasped his hand into hers, and she took him to the altar and stood to face him. She searched his eyes so deeply and hadn't seen him so weak and helpless like this before.

"Many years ago, Junior, we both stood on this altar. Remember our vows? Remember you whispered in my ear never to leave me. I told you I wouldn't, that is the reason I'm here. I am your wife, Junior, and I am meant to be with you forever, through the good and the bad times. We've had good times and also bad times, why would I leave you now? All I want from you is to know that we can

61

be happy together with or without a child. She held his face. "remember when you told me I was a miracle in your life?... our children will be our miracles too. Trust God with me because I know it won't be long... "

"Who are you, Cherish... " Junior was weak with her words.

"The one who vowed to be with you till the end." She smiles through her thin tears

"God, I love you so much, Cherish." He hugs her again.

"So, will you come back home with me?" Cherish searched his eyes.

"I have no other place to call home." He plants a soft kiss on her lips, and they were both on their way back home.

Epilogue

Junior and Cherish were on the sofa watching a late-night movie. Cherish was resting on his shoulders when she felt the movement.

"Junior, junior, it moved again… don't miss it this time, touch it." She gently placed his palm on the side of the stomach. Both felt the movement of their child

"I can feel him… I can feel him." Junior placed his head on her belly.

"I can feel him growing each day inside of me… "

"What do you think it's saying now by this movement?"

"Thank you, Pappy for believing in me." She laughed. They both laughed "The movement has stopped." He slowly removes his head from her stomach, "I think he's sleeping."

Cherish rests on his shoulders again, "In six months, you'd be a dad, "You finally got your miracle."

Junior tilts his wife's face to him, looking into her eyes, "Cherish, you were the miracle I needed. Thank you for not leaving me."

Cherish tickles his nose with hers, "I love you too. Always will," she smiles. "We missed a whole lot in our movie."

"Movie can wait, but this can't." He gently plants a kiss on her belly.

About the Author

Gabriel is a psychologist with a background in Sociology, he has a wide range of experience in a variety of areas, including supporting young offenders, prison outreach, restorative justice, and helping people recover from substance abuse.

He has a BSc in Sociology, Bowen University, Osun, Nigeria, PGD in Community Relations, Pan Atlantic University, Lagos, Nigeria; MSc in criminology with forensic psychology at Middlesex University, London, United Kingdom.

He also offers psychological intervention programs and counselling for individuals, and married people.

Thank you

I will like to say a big Thank you for buying a copy of this book. And I do hope you enjoyed reading it.

If you love and cherish this book, then, you do have my permission to buy a copy as a gift for a friend, or a family member.

If you are interested in getting to know what I am up to at any point in time or would simply like to say a quick hello, kindly send me an email at gabrieloluseyi_akinyemi@yahoo.co.uk and I will gladly write back.

Cheers.

Printed in Great Britain
by Amazon